THE

THREE LITTLE PIGS

Illustrated
by
RENE CLOKE

AWARD PUBLICATIONS — LONDON

THE THREE LITTLE PIGS

Three little pigs, Grunter, Porker and Squeaky, lived with a number of other pigs in a cosy farmyard.

"This sty is too crowded," Grunter grumbled, "let's go out and seek adventures in the big world."

"Yes," agreed Porker, "good idea!"

"Wee, wee, wee!" squealed Squeaky; this meant "Yes, yes yes!" for he didn't want to be left behind.

So they packed their belongings, said good-bye to their friends and left the farm.

"We will each build a little house," suggested Grunter, as they walked down the lane, " and visit each other when we want to talk about our adventures."

The first person they met was a man carrying a load of straw.

"I will build a nice house with that straw" thought Grunter, who was rather stupid.

The man was quite glad to sell the heavy load, so Grunter built himself a pretty little house while Porker and Squeaky went on their way.

That evening, a wolf came along the road and called out to Grunter through the window.

."Let me in, I love fat little pigs!"

But Grunter kept the door shut.

"I shall blow and blow till I blow the house down," cried the wolf and with three great puffs he blew the house of straw to pieces.

Grunter escaped by running across the field and hiding under the hedge.

When Porker and Squeaky left Grunter, they saw a boy gathering sticks.

"I should like to buy your bundle of sticks to build a house," said Porker.

"Certainly," said the boy.

So Porker took the sticks and built himself a stick house.

When the wolf came through the wood, he saw Porker at the window.

"Open the door!" he cried.

"Oh, no!" answered Porker, "I don't like wolves."

"Then I'll blow and I'll blow and I'll blow the house down," cried the wolf.

He blew seven great puffs and the house of sticks fell to bits.

Porker managed to scuttle out of the back door and hide behind a tree.

Squeaky walked along the road by himself, while Porker was building his house of sticks and there, by the side of the road, he saw a man wheeling a load of bricks.

Squeaky was the youngest pig but he was the cleverest and he decided to build his house of bricks and a fine strong house it was.

The wolf was feeling very hungry by now, two fat little pigs had escaped and he was still looking for his supper.

"Let me in!" he cried to Squeaky.

"It's too late," answered Squeaky, "I'm just going to bed."

"Very well," replied the wolf, "I shall blow and blow till I blow the house down!"

But although he blew and blew, the brick house was too strong to blow over.

Squeaky just laughed.

"Little pig," called the wolf at last, "if you are fond of turnips, I can show you a field full of them. I will call for you in the morning at nine o'clock and we will go there together."

"Many thanks," said Squeaky and he rolled over and went to sleep.

The little pig awoke early and was up by seven o'clock.

He ran to the turnip field and had a good breakfast there.

When the wolf came to call for him, Squeaky waved from the window.

"I couldn't wait for you, Mr Wolf," he cried, "I was too hungry for my breakfast."

So the wolf had to think of another way to catch him.

"Let us go to the orchard," he suggested, "I will call for you at eight o'clock and we will have a fine feast of apples."

"Thank you," said Squeaky, "that's a fine idea."

But Squeaky was up at six and ran to the orchard.

When the wolf arrived, he was sitting in a tree.

"Hullo," called out the little pig, "I was too hungry to wait for you, here's a fine apple — catch it!"

He threw an apple to the wolf but it rolled away and, while the wolf was chasing it, Squeaky climbed down and ran home.

13

The next day the wolf visited Squeaky's little brick house again.

"Have you heard the news?" he asked Squeaky, "there is to be a grand Fair on the Common.

It would be fun if we could go together in the afternoon."

"Thank you," said Squeaky, "it certainly would."

But the little pig went to the Fair in the morning and had a lovely time on the swings and roundabouts.

He met a great many animals he knew and they had a jolly time together.

In the afternoon, Squeaky
decided that it was time to leave
the Fair.

His pockets were full of good things that
he had won and he was carrying a butter
churn that he had bought at a farm stall.

As he reached the top of the hill he saw the wolf making his way to the Fair.

"I must think of a plan quickly to escape," said Squeaky to himself, "or he will certainly catch me."

But there seemed to be nowhere to hide.

Then he thought of the butter churn and in he jumped before the wolf caught sight of him.

But as the churn was round, it started rolling down the hill — the little pig was very surprised and so was the wolf!

"Help!" he yelled as he jumped out of the way, "what can this horrible thing be?"

He was so frightened that he ran off as fast as he could go.

When the butter churn stopped at the bottom of the hill, Squeaky climbed out and held his sides with laughter.

"Ha! ha! ha!" he cried, "that trick worked well!"

He picked up the churn and carried it home.

To his delight, he found Grunter and Porker waiting for him on the doorstep.

"You have built a fine strong house," Grunter cried, "the wolf blew down my house of straw."

"Yes, and he blew down my house of sticks," wailed Porker.

"Never mind," said Squeaky, "we will all live here and make a plan to catch the wolf."

Before long, the wolf came and knocked at the door.

"Save me!" he cried, "I have been chased by a horrible round thing which tried to knock me down!"

"Were you indeed?" answered Squeaky from the window, "that must have been me inside the butter churn; what a good thing you got out of my way — I might have hurt you!"

"I will catch you yet!" growled the furious wolf, "I shall climb down the chimney and then you will stop laughing, for I shall eat you for supper!"

Grunter and Porker shook with fright but Squeaky was thinking hard.

"Quick!" he whispered, "help me to put this cooking pot of boiling water on the fire."
The three little pigs put the pot over the fire just as the wolf came down the chimney.

Into the boiling water he plopped
and Squeaky put on the lid and they all
held it down.

So that was the end of the wolf.

"Now we'll have a grand party," said
Squeaky and they asked all their animal
friends to tea.

Later, they collected some more bricks and built enough rooms onto the strong little house for all three pigs to live together in safety.